LET'S GO!

W9-CFK-287

Bike Riding

Written by Caleb Burroughs
Illustrated by Louise Gardner

ISBN-13: 978-1-4127-9182-3
ISBN-10: 1-4127-9182-0

8 7 6 5 4 3 2 1

pi kids **publications international, ltd.**

Hi! My name is Gina. I just had a big birthday party. There were colorful balloons and games to play. We ate cake and ice cream, too.

My friends brought me lots of great gifts. But the best gift was from my mommy and daddy. Can you guess what was in the wrapping paper?

That's right, a new bike!

The next day, I couldn't wait to try out my new bike.

"Be careful," Mommy said. I promised her I would.

"What are these little wheels for?" I asked.

"Those are training wheels," said Daddy. "They keep you from falling while you learn to ride your bike."

That sounded good to me.

Before I could try riding, I put on my helmet. That's to keep me from getting hurt.

It was kind of hard climbing onto my bike at first.

"You'll get used to it, Gina," Daddy said. "Now put your feet on the pedals."

My feet just reached the pedals. I couldn't wait to zoom around like a big kid!

"Ready, steady, go!" Daddy shouted. He gave me a push and I raced down the sidewalk.

"Whee!" I yelled. The wind rushed past my face as I pedaled faster. It felt great!

"Stop when you get to the end of the sidewalk," Daddy called. I practiced doing the brakes. That's how you stop. Then I practiced turning.

After a few days of practice, Daddy said I was riding really well. "I think you're doing so well that we can take the training wheels off," he said.

So we brought my bike into the garage, where he keeps his tools. I helped by handing Daddy the tools he needed.

"Are you ready to ride your two-wheeler?" he asked me.

At first I wasn't very good at riding with just two wheels. I fell down — a lot!

Every time I fell, Daddy was there to help me get back up. "Falling is how you learn," he said. Then he would kiss my boo-boos and make them feel better.

Daddy was right. Each time I got back on my bike, I made it a little farther without falling.

Then, all of a sudden, I was riding on two wheels and I wasn't falling—just like a big kid!

"Look at you go!" Daddy called. "I'm so proud of you!"

I was proud, too. I rode around the block again and again. Once I got going, I didn't want to stop.

"Look at me!" I yelled as I rode past. "I'm really doing it!"

Now I ride all around the neighborhood with my friends. I can ride really fast and do all kinds of neat tricks.

I sure do love my new bike!